To MY Little Dragons.
Thank you for making me a storyteller for real!
And to my husband, Gregory,
there is no one like you in all the world.
Thank you for your patience and support.

Special thanks to
Kathy Rowe, Samantha Wright & Jason Sturgill

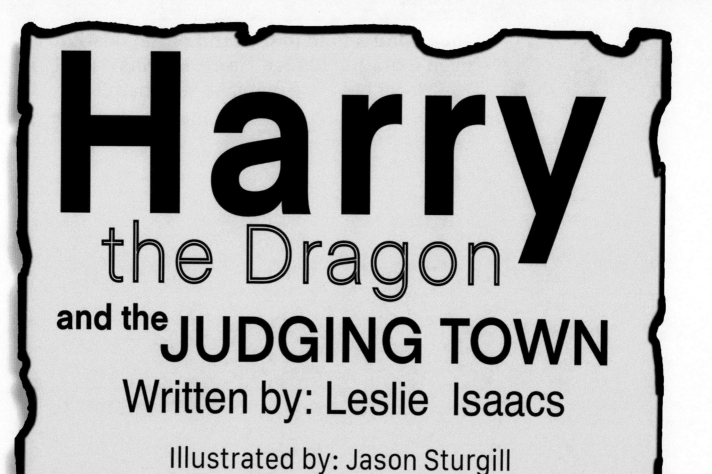

Harry
the Dragon
and the JUDGING TOWN

Written by: Leslie Isaacs

Illustrated by: Jason Sturgill

Once upon a time in the land of Kay-Ma-Zoo lived a dragon named Harry. He was called Harry because, well, he was hairy!

Harry loved cornbread.

As he was flying into town the people heard him coming! They began to scream, "Run! RUN! Here comes Harry the Dragon and he will eat you! RUN! RUN!"

When Harry got to town he found the streets empty. The only people in town were the shop owners because they could not leave their stores.

Harry found the grocery store and went in.

The man behind the counter said in a shaky voice, "Hello". Harry greeted him with a nice, "Hello. How are you today?" The man squeaked out a "Fine….. I MUST go to the back!" and ran to the back of the store. Harry thought that to be strange but began to go down the isles in search for his supplies.

He found everything he needed and headed to the counter to checkout. But when he reached the counter he found a note that read,

"Please! Leave your money on the counter!"

Harry once again found this odd but left his $2.32 and went home happily with his ingredients for his cornbread.

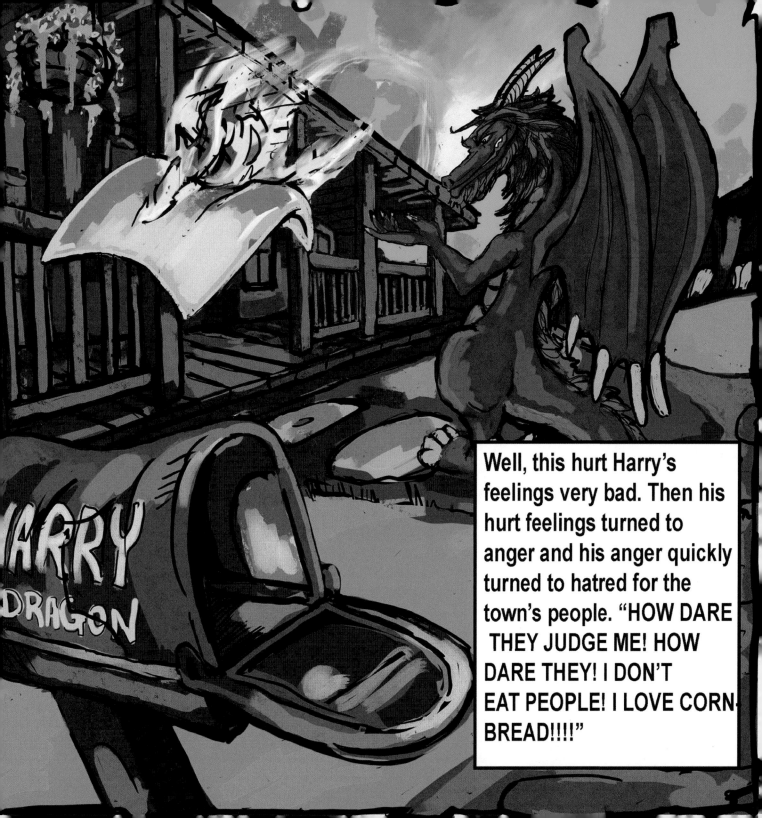

Well, this hurt Harry's feelings very bad. Then his hurt feelings turned to anger and his anger quickly turned to hatred for the town's people. "HOW DARE THEY JUDGE ME! HOW DARE THEY! I DON'T EAT PEOPLE! I LOVE CORN-BREAD!!!!"

One day while he was working around in his house he heard someone cry for help. "Is there anyone there?! HELP! HELP! I've fallen down in the well!"

Harry quickly went to the well to help the person out.

Harry yelled down and said, "Don't worry. I'm here and I'll get a rope to pull you out." When Harry had almost gotten the old man pulled out, the old man looked at Harry, screamed and let go of the rope!

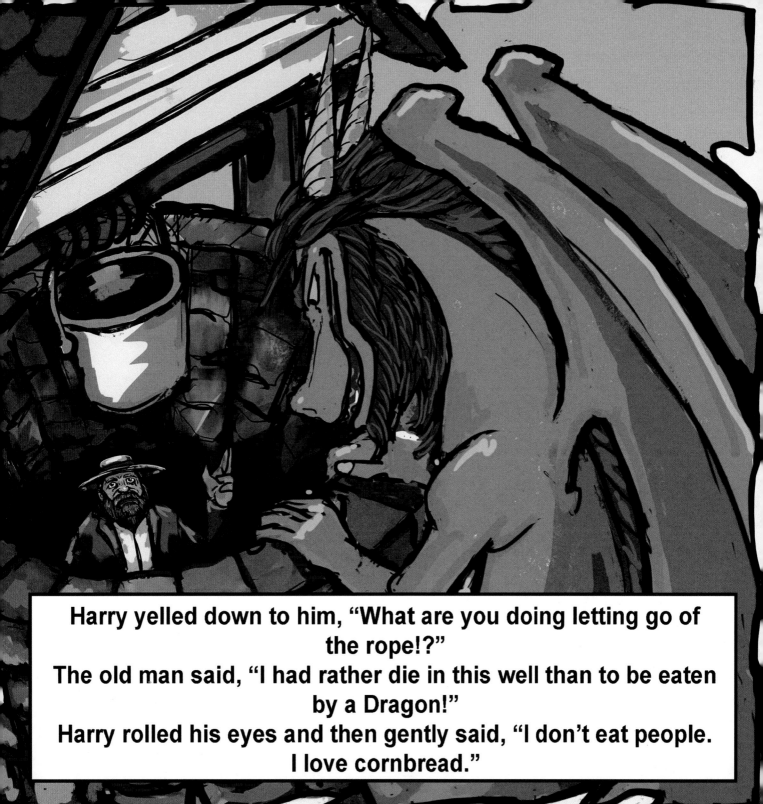

Harry yelled down to him, "What are you doing letting go of the rope!?"
The old man said, "I had rather die in this well than to be eaten by a Dragon!"
Harry rolled his eyes and then gently said, "I don't eat people. I love cornbread."

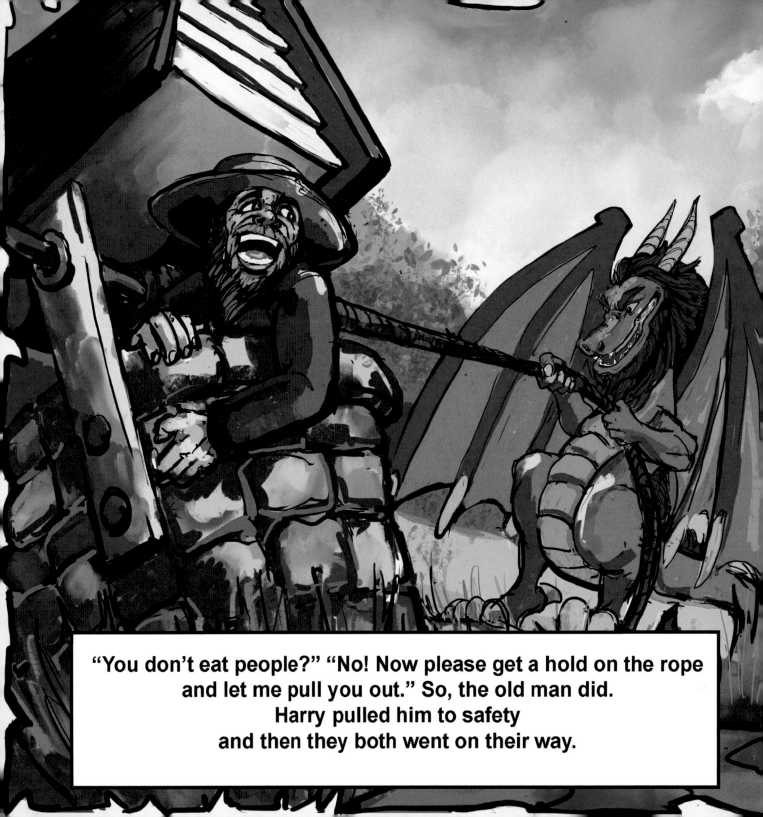

"You don't eat people?" "No! Now please get a hold on the rope and let me pull you out." So, the old man did.
Harry pulled him to safety
and then they both went on their way.

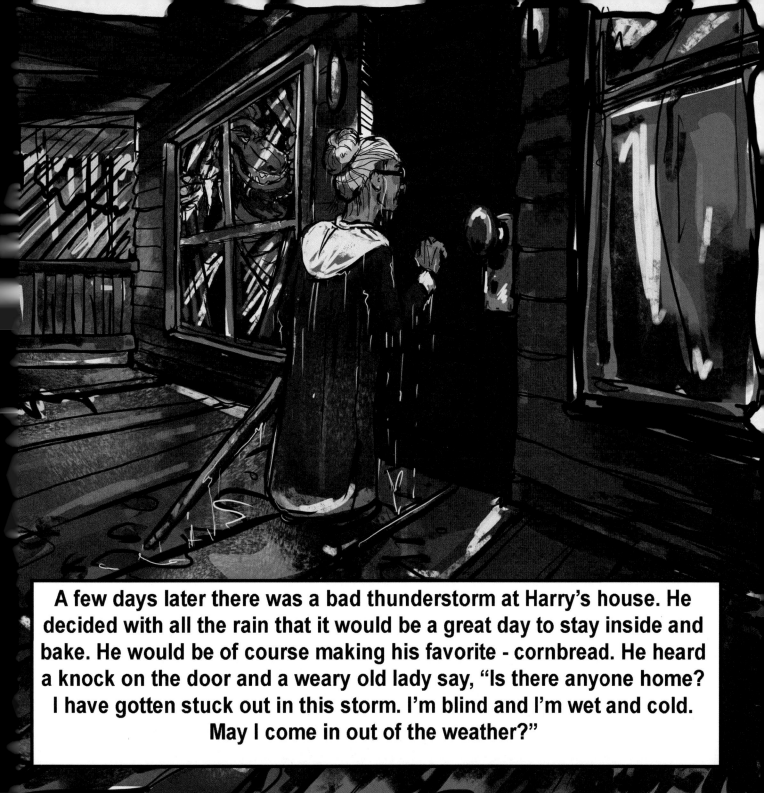

A few days later there was a bad thunderstorm at Harry's house. He decided with all the rain that it would be a great day to stay inside and bake. He would be of course making his favorite - cornbread. He heard a knock on the door and a weary old lady say, "Is there anyone home? I have gotten stuck out in this storm. I'm blind and I'm wet and cold. May I come in out of the weather?"

Harry quickly went to the door to let the little old lady inside. He lead her to a chair close by the fire so she could get warm. He got her a blanket and some hot tea. She could smell the cornbread baking and asked Harry what it was.
"I'm baking cornbread. Would you like some?"
"Oh yes!"
He brought her a buttered piece and she enjoyed it.

Once she had finished she said to Harry, "My child, I am an old blind lady and I don't recognize your voice. Do you mind if I feel your face and hands to get a better idea of what you look like?"
"Of course." Harry said and gently knelt beside her.
As quickly as she felt his long hairy face she screamed with freight! "YOU ARE HARRY THE DRAGON! YOU WILL EAT ME! PLEASE DON'T EAT ME!!!"
Harry rolled his eyes and took a breathe. "I don't eat people."
"You don't eat people?"
"No, I don't eat people. I LOVE CORNBREAD!"

The little old lady heard the rain stop and decided it was time to leave.
Harry lead her back to the road toward town and off she went.

The next morning Harry awoke to the best smell. He sat up in his bed with his eyes still shut but his nose stuck into the air sniffing away. "Sniff, Sniff" He got up and began to walk through his house with his nose in the air and his eyes shut tight. "YUMMY! WHAT A SMELL!!"

He went to his front door and opened it. He couldn't believe his eyes! There on his porch were pones and pones of cornbread! And in his yard were the towns people of Kay-Ma-Zoo with a huge banner that read:
"WE ARE SORRY HARRY! WE JUDGED YOU! PLEASE FORGIVE US!"
Right then and there something wonderful happened. He forgave them and Harry's anger and hatred melted away like the snow.

THE END
(For now)

Harry's Cornbread

This is a great recipe for kids to help mix!
USE CAUTION AS THIS RECIPE REQUIRES A HOT SKILLET AND HOT OIL

Ingredients:
1 ½ Cups self-rising flour
1 ½ Cups cornmeal
1 egg
1 ¾ Cups milk
2 Tbsp Oil

Instructions:
1. **Preheat oven to 350°**
2. **Place the oil in the skillet and place the pan in the oven while preheating**
3. **Combine the ingredients into a bowl and mix till combined**
4. **Take the hot skillet out of the oven and pour in the batter slowly as the batter will fry on the outside from the hot pan and hot oil**
5. **Return skillet and batter to the oven and cook for about 25 minutes or until a toothpick comes out clean**
6. **Serve warm**

Pro Tips:
1. **If the skillet doesn't seem to fry the edges when you pour in the batter it will not hurt the cornbread. If you prefer this to happen next time, just leave the skillet in the oven a little longer. This will leave a nice crust and makes the cornbread even better.**
2. **The top of the cornbread will crack during cooking. So, if you want the top to be a bit browner, just turn on your oven's broiler and keep the cornbread under the broiler until your desired brownness.**
3. **For extra goodness add butter and/or jelly to a slice.**

Made in the USA
Monee, IL
08 September 2021